KU-499-104

Mr Grinling was a lighthouse keeper. He and Mrs Grinling lived with their cat, Hamish, in the little white cottage perched high on the cliffs.

It was nearly Christmas and Mr Grinling's great-nephew, George, was coming to stay.

"We'll make it the best Christmas ever for George and for you," said Mrs Grinling as she bustled around the kitchen.

Mr Grinling sighed. "Sometimes I forget it's my last Christmas as the lighthouse keeper."

"Perhaps we could have Christmas Day in the lighthouse," suggested Mrs Grinling.

"Mrs G, I think that's the best idea you've ever had. Christmas Day in my lighthouse, how perfectly splendid."

George arrived.

"Wowee," he exclaimed. "Christmas Day in the lighthouse."

"I must write to Father Christmas so he knows where I am. Can you help me please, Uncle G?" he asked.

They wrote the letter together.

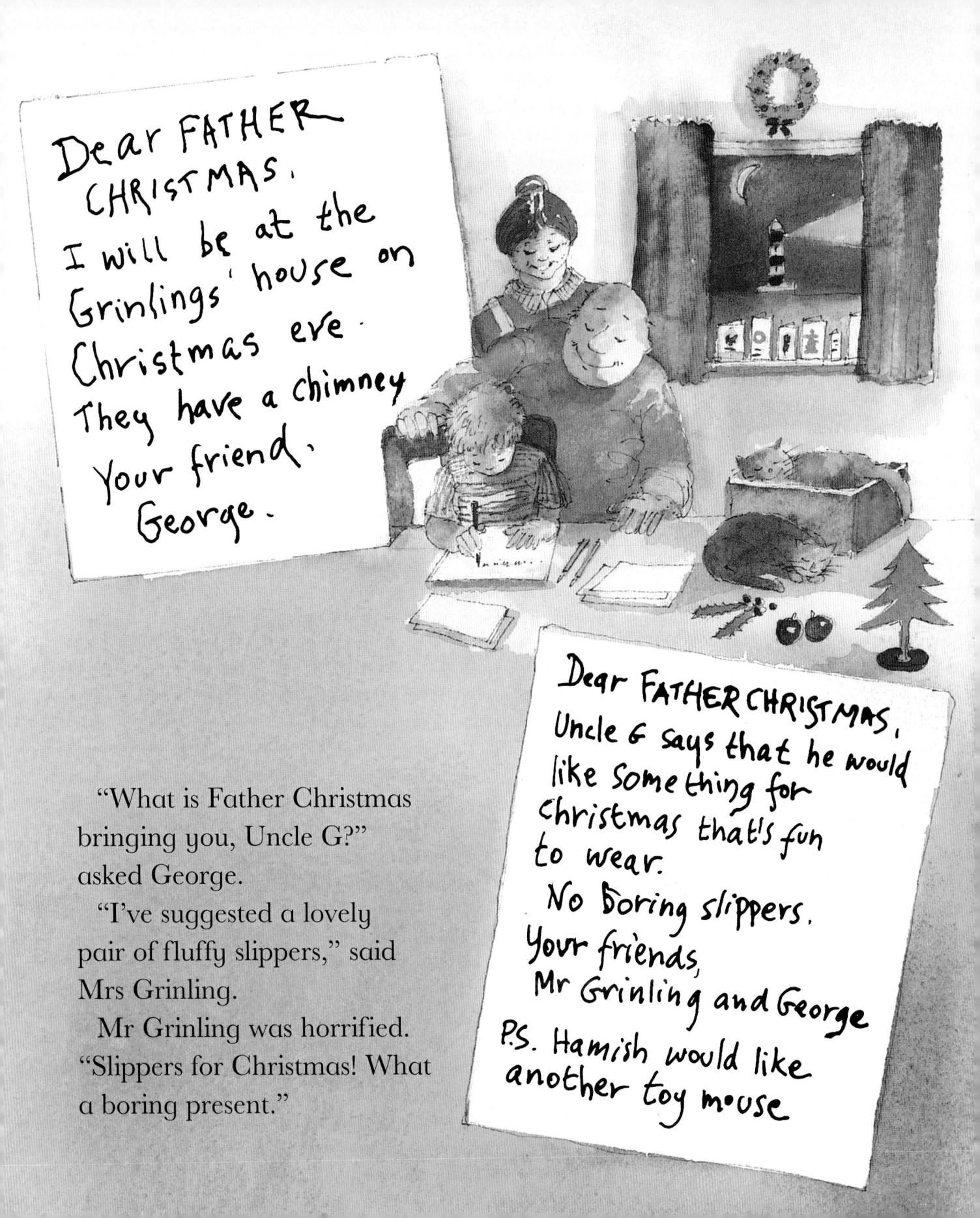

"What is Father Christmas bringing you, Uncle G?" asked George.

"I've suggested a lovely pair of fluffy slippers," said Mrs Grinling.

Mr Grinling was horrified. "Slippers for Christmas! What a boring present."

On Christmas Eve Mrs Grinling was so busy that Mr Grinling and George had to make their own lunch.

They packed everything into the boat and rowed out to the lighthouse.

"See you tonight," called Mrs Grinling. "Don't be late."

The Lighthouse Keeper's Christmas

Ronda & David Armitage

013738750 6

To retired lighthouse keepers everywhere

First published in 2002 by Scholastic Ltd
Euston House, 24 Eversholt Street
London NW1 1DB
a division of Scholastic Ltd
www.scholastic.co.uk
London ~ New York ~ Toronto ~ Sydney ~ Auckland
Mexico City ~ New Delhi ~ Hong Kong

Text copyright © 2002 Ronda Armitage
Illustrations copyright © 2002 David Armitage

ISBN 978 0439 98221 4

All rights reserved
Printed in China

10 9

The moral rights of Ronda Armitage and David Armitage have been asserted.

Papers used by Scholastic Children's Books are made from wood grown in sustainable forests.

There was lots to do.

Mr Grinling cleaned,

George polished,

and Hamish slept.

At last the lighthouse shone like a new pin.

"George," said Mr Grinling, "you're the best lighthouse helper I've ever had. I think you've earned yourself a splendiferous lunch."

Look how that lighthouse gleams and glows.

They sat outside in the wintry sunshine. A lone grey seal basked nearby.

"I wish I could help at the lighthouse all the time," said George. "Will you be sad when you're not a lighthouse keeper any more?"

"Yes and no," said Mr Grinling. "On the days when the wind howls each way, every way, and my fingers are so cold I can't even feel them, then I won't be sad. But on the other days, when the sun shines and little boats frolic on that blue sea – yes, George, *then* I will be sad. But Sam is looking after the lighthouse so I can come and visit whenever I like."

Later, they put up the Christmas decorations and sang Christmas carols together, very loudly.

They were so busy that Mr Grinling didn't notice the darkening sky.

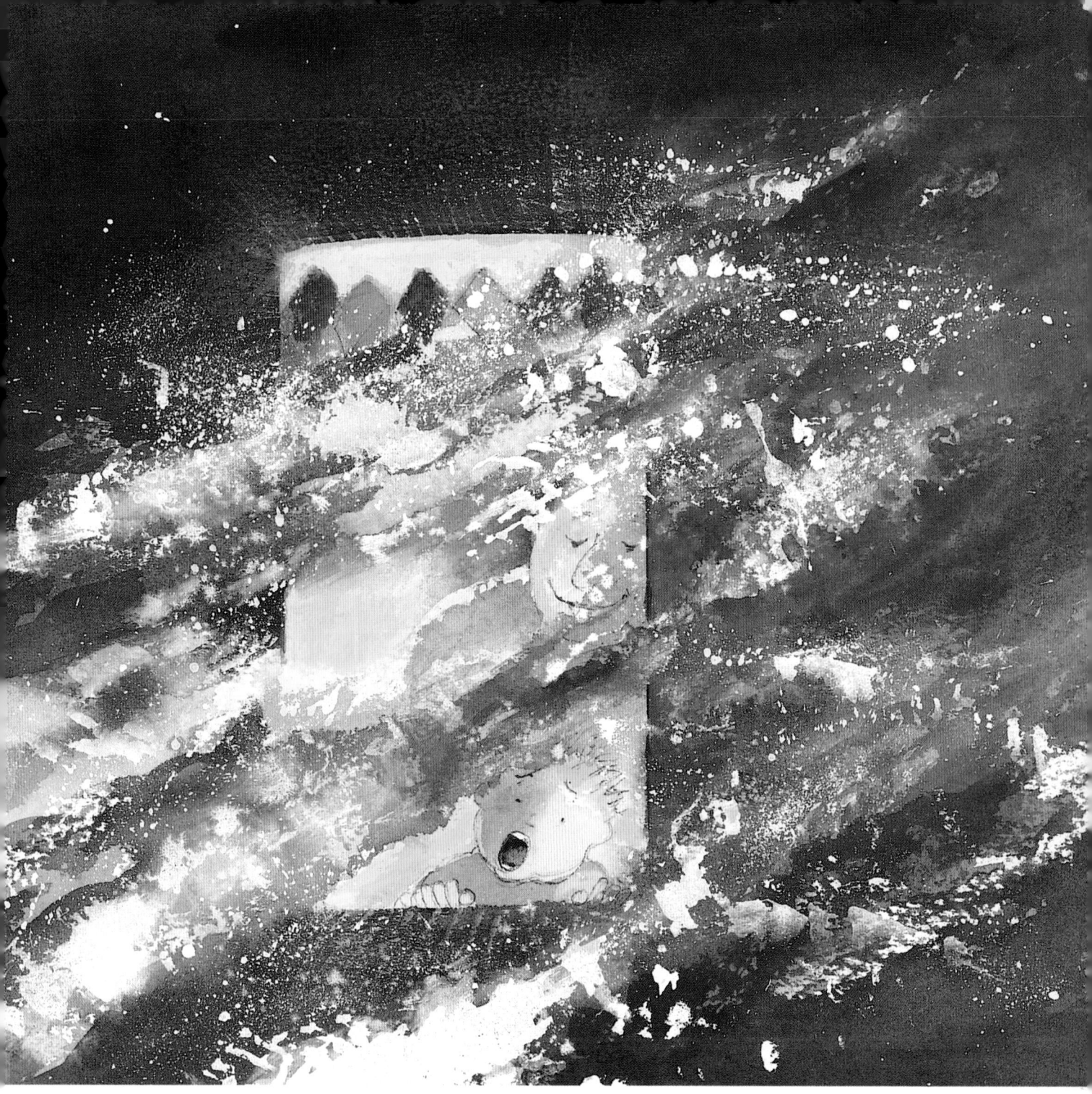

A wave splashed the window. "What's that?" asked George.
"Well, well," said Mr Grinling, "I think we're in for a storm."
"I don't like storms," said George. "Could we go home now, please?"

But when they opened the lighthouse door they could see the little dinghy tossed high by the waves. Mr Grinling tried to reach it with the boat hook but the dinghy was too far away.

George began to cry.

"Now George," said Mr Grinling. "No tears. We've got plenty of water already. You're a very lucky boy."

George stopped crying. "Am I?" he said.

"Absolutely," announced Mr Grinling. "You're probably the luckiest boy in the whole world because you're in the middle of a Christmas Eve Lighthouse Adventure. As a special treat you can turn on the light."

George cheered up enough to feel hungry.

"Do people have tea when they're in the middle of an adventure?"

Mr Grinling rummaged in the lunch basket. It was quite empty.

"They do," he said. "But they ring Mrs Grinling first."

The wind was so fierce that George and Mr Grinling tied themselves to the rail as they waited for the food basket to arrive in the usual way.

It turned and twisted down the wire. But the wind was hungry too. With an almighty gust it threw the basket high in the air.

The lid dropped open and George and Mr Grinling watched the seagulls dive on their tea as it fell to the ground.

"Never mind," said Mr Grinling. "There must be something in the cupboard. I'll see what I can rustle up."

He found a very small tin of baked beans, some sardines, one shrivelled potato and a packet of chocolate biscuits.

"What a feast," he declared. "Just right for a Christmas Eve adventure."

After they'd eaten, Mr Grinling made up some beds. Still the wind howled, still the waves roared, and thunder clouds filled the air.

"Listen to that weather," said Mr Grinling. "This adventure is getting more exciting all the time."

"I always have a story before I go to sleep, Uncle G," said George.

"Of course," said Mr Grinling. "Now let me see. I know, I'll tell you about the time when Father Christmas forgot to come to our house on Christmas Eve."

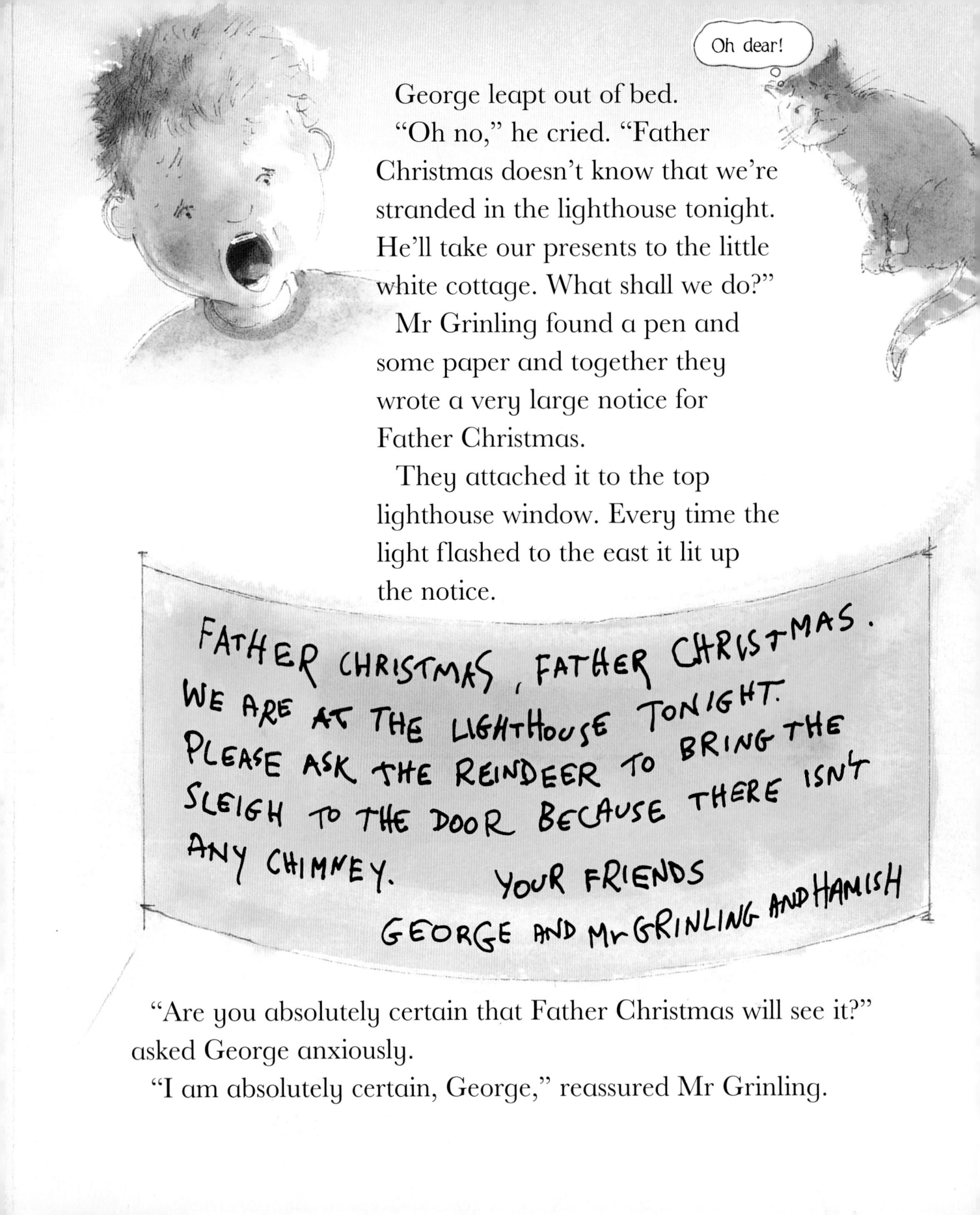

George leapt out of bed.

"Oh no," he cried. "Father Christmas doesn't know that we're stranded in the lighthouse tonight. He'll take our presents to the little white cottage. What shall we do?"

Mr Grinling found a pen and some paper and together they wrote a very large notice for Father Christmas.

They attached it to the top lighthouse window. Every time the light flashed to the east it lit up the notice.

"Are you absolutely certain that Father Christmas will see it?" asked George anxiously.

"I am absolutely certain, George," reassured Mr Grinling.

"But what about our Christmas stockings?" asked George.

"Mmmm," mused Mr Grinling. "If I can just remember where I put them…"

He found two enormous yellow socks.

"I knitted these myself."

They left the socks and a chocolate biscuit by the lighthouse door, then Mr Grinling tucked George back into bed.

George woke in the middle of the night. Outside, the world was quiet and still again. Except for a slight tinkling noise.

He tip-toed to the window. It was the night before Christmas, and the moon shone dark in the sky.

"You found us, Father Christmas," he whispered.

George was first up in the morning. He and Hamish peered out the window. Snow lay all around, even on the grey seals.

"Wowee," George exclaimed. "It's a proper Christmas after all, presents AND snow."

Then George's face dropped.

"I can't see the little white cottage, or the path. They're covered in snow. Maybe Auntie G is stranded now. How will she get to us for Christmas?"

"Goodness gracious me, George, don't you worry," chuckled Mr Grinling. "Mrs G is full of good ideas. I'm sure she'll think of something, just you wait and see."

They had two chocolate biscuits each for breakfast while they opened some of their presents.

At last Mrs Grinling rang.

"As it's your final meal as the lighthouse keeper, I'm sending Christmas dinner in the basket. Don't worry about me, I'll get there somehow."

"Mrs G, you're wonderful," grinned Mr Grinling.

George and Mr Grinling waited patiently as the basket slid down the wire.

George shook his fist at the scavenging seagulls. "Clear off, you pesky birds! Leave our Christmas dinner alone."

The basket stopped. Mr Grinling shook the wire but the basket wouldn't move.

His tummy rumbled. He was sure he could smell roast potatoes.

Tom, Bert and Fred hovered above the basket.

"No, no, no!" shouted George and Mr Grinling. But the seagulls ignored them.

"Squawk, squawk!" they cried, and all together they dived.

The basket jerked and wobbled, then slid down the wire.

"Well I never," exclaimed Mr Grinling. "Those seagulls, they're full of surprises."

George and Mr Grinling unpacked the Christmas dinner.

"Look," said Mr Grinling. "Mrs G has sent some little extra food packets." He read the labels. "Happy Christmas to those pesky seagulls, Tom, Bert and Fred."

A speedboat circled the lighthouse. George waved and called.

"Uncle G, Uncle G, it's alright! Auntie G is here and Sam's come too."

"I knew she'd get here somehow," smiled Mr Grinling.

Sam was carrying a large sack.

"More presents," he said, "from all the people in the village."

And he read from the biggest card Mr Grinling had ever seen. "Happy Retirement to the best lighthouse keeper in the world."

Mr Grinling wiped his right eye.

"Now, now, Uncle G," said George firmly. "No tears. We've got plenty of water already."

"Quite right, George," said Mr Grinling. "This is no time to be sad. You and I have had the best Christmas lighthouse adventure ever."

"And now we're going to have the best Christmas dinner ever," said Mrs Grinling.

It was almost dark by the time they finished eating.

"Time for your last light, Mr G," announced Sam.

"Come on everybody," said Mr Grinling. "Let's turn it on together."

The light beamed brightly and clearly out to sea. From out of the darkness all around came the sound of hooting and tooting from the ships and boats.

"That's the best present a lighthouse keeper could have," said Mr Grinling. "Thank you, thank you everybody."